ALANi

and the

Giant Kelp Elf

ALANi
and the
Giant Kelp Elf

WRITTEN AND ILLUSTRATED BY

Gayle and Tom Joliet

Contents

From beneath a thick cover of green vines a child-sized, webbed hand reached out, placed a nautilus shell necklace on a tree stump and retreated back underground to wait.

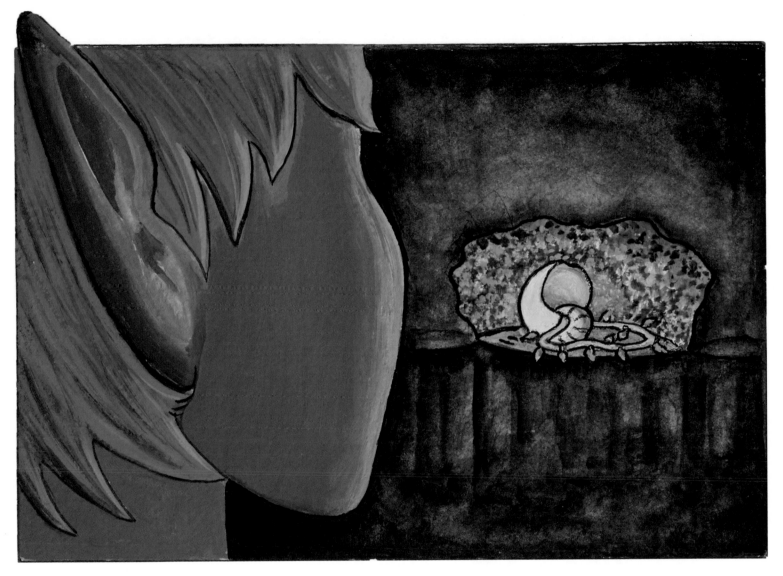

Eager eyes peered through a small gap in the vines
to see if the garden girl would
find her magic gift.

Alani pointed the garden hose high up to the sky and watched the spray as it sparkled in the afternoon sun. She had the Garden Park, in the little village of Laguna Beach, all to herself... well, except for Alley, the garden cat, who was always there to greet her. It was her favorite time to come, on her way home from school, when the adults were still at work and her classmates had gone home to play.

To Alani, this was a MAGICAL place. Ever since she was a little girl riding in her father's backpack, she had watched it change from a weedy vacant lot into a beautiful garden. Village neighbors had cleared the land, built wooden planter boxes for each family, and filled them with soil. Then, like magic, the tiny seeds they poked into the ground had grown into vegetables, fruits and flowers.

When Alani had finished watering her family's garden plot, she saw that the vine-covered mound nearby needed water, too, so she turned the hose on it. As she watched rainbows dancing in the sprinkling water she noticed that the vines below seemed to move.

"Hmm," Alani wondered, *"could there be rabbits or squirrels building a home underneath?"*

Just in case, worried that she might flood them out, Alani pointed the nozzle higher up the hillside and watched as a butterfly darted in and out of the spray.

Suddenly, the vines moved again, and a bright sparkle caught her eye.

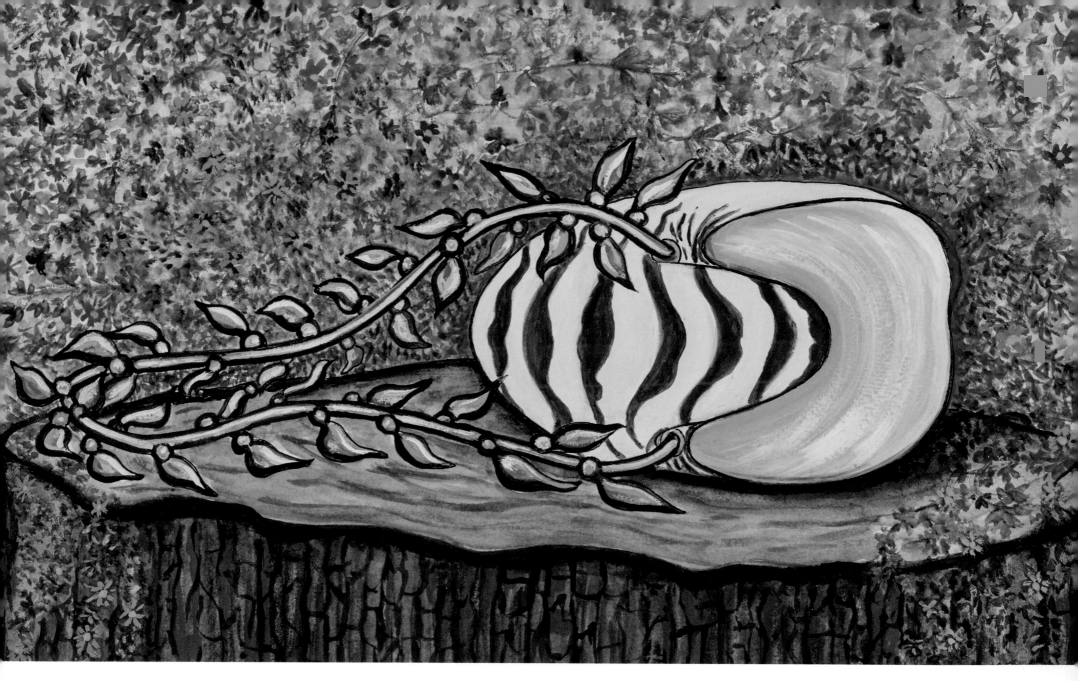

"Wow!" she cried.

Looking closer, she was startled to see a beautiful nautilus shell shining in the sunlight. Quick as a wink, Alani shut off the water and dropped the hose.

"How strange," she thought. She had never seen anything like it before. The shell was attached to a rubbery seaweed stem. It looked like a necklace!

12

Amazed, she picked it up and placed the hollow of the shell next to her ear, expecting to hear the sound of ocean waves...

but this time,
she was greeted with a voice!

"Hello, Alani!" it said.

She jumped back and looked into the shell. *"How can a voice be coming out of this?"*

But the shell kept talking, *"My name is Kelfie. I am a giant Kelp Elf, and..."*

"You're a GIANT? I thought giants were only in fairy tales!"

*"No, no! I am not a giant! I LIVE in the giant kelp forest...
Macro-cystis-py-RIF-era."*

"Mac-a-ro-ni WHAT?" she asked.

"No! Not macaroni," he laughed... *"Macro-cystis-py-rif-era... It is the
scientific name for the giant kelp that grows in our undersea gardens.
You probably call it seaweed."*

"Oh,"
Alani replied,

"I've been learning about that at school.

Aren't the giant kelp forests in trouble?"

"Yes!"
Kelfie answered,

"That is why I need to talk to you.

If you put the necklace on and look under the vines, you will be able to see me.

It is MAGIC!"

Alani carefully pulled the kelp leaf necklace over her head, lifted the vines and peered down. Sure enough, there was a pointy-eared, elf-like child about her size, smiling up at her from inside a tunnel. He had webbed hands and feet, was dressed in seaweed leaves, and wore an identical shell necklace.

"Wow! How did you get here?"

"I hiked up this secret lava tunnel that connects the ocean to this mound," Kelfie explained. *"Our Elf Clan has been watching from the kelp canopy for a long time. You and the other villagers work so hard to care for your land garden, we think you will also care about our sea forest. Especially you, Alani. You come and work here almost every day!"*

Alani smiled, *"I love working in this garden. I think it's fun!"*

"That is why we chose to contact YOU with the magic necklace. My grandfather, our Clan leader, is asking if the villagers can help us. The problem is that sea urchins are destroying our kelp forest. They eat kelp, and that is usually okay. But people have caught too many big fish that eat the urchins. Now there are too many urchins. They gnaw at the roots, called holdfasts, causing the giant kelp to drift away."

"Besides that," Kelfie continued, "trash and poisons that flow into the sea kill the plants and animals. Do you think there is anything the villagers can do to help us? It is so unhealthy that we have to leave our homes."

"It must be VERY serious if you can't even live here anymore.
I'll see what I can find out."

"Excellent!" Kelfie replied. "Can we meet again tomorrow at the same time, same place? I need to get back in the ocean now. With the magic necklace, I can breathe and talk on land, but only for a short time."

"Okay, I'll look for the necklace tomorrow!" Alani said. As soon as she handed it back to him, the magic was gone, and Kelfie disappeared. Alani rolled up the hose, slung her backpack over her shoulder, and headed up the wooden stairs.

"Meow!" purred Alley Cat.

When Alani bent down to pet her, she noticed a wrinkled poster lying under Alley's front paws. Picking it up, she saw a picture of seaweed on the paper.

"What's this?" It was a plan to create a *"Bluebelt"* to protect the ocean. There would be a meeting soon at City Hall.

"Kelfie should see this," she whispered to Alley. She looked back at the mound, but the necklace was gone. Kelfie was already sliding back down the tunnel and swimming to his home in the giant kelp forest. She rolled up the poster and headed the few blocks to her house.

Meanwhile, back in his underwater home, Kelfie's grandfather was helping the Kelp Elves to pack their things.

"The magic necklace worked, Grandfather!" Kelfie explained. *"Alani will try to find out if the villagers can help us. She is meeting me again tomorrow."*

"Good job, Kelfie!" Grandfather replied. *"Maybe there is hope for us after all. Remember when I told you how the villagers saved the plants and animals on land? I think they can do the same for the ocean."*

Grandfather had told the Elf children stories about growing up in the giant kelp forest. When he was a young boy body-surfing the waves close to shore, he had watched the land become more and more crowded.

He began to worry that concrete and tall buildings might someday cover the hillsides and destroy the homes of the plants and animals that lived there.

Wearing his magic shell necklace, he heard the people of Laguna Beach talking and learned that many of them were worried, too.

Fortunately, those caring villagers convinced their city leaders to pass new laws to protect the land. These laws prevented more tall buildings and turned parts of Laguna into what they called a Greenbelt.

Grandfather was relieved that the people had spoken up, and he stopped worrying about the land.

But now, years later, he had a new concern. This time, it was for the ocean, his home beneath the sea. He hoped Alani's news would mean it wasn't too late.

When Alani got home, she found her mom, Carly, at the kitchen table.

"Mom!" Alani cried, "Look what I found under Alley Cat's paws! Have you ever heard of the Laguna Bluebelt?"

"Oh, yes!" Carly replied. "I'm going to that City Hall meeting to speak in favor of a 'Bluebelt' to make Laguna's coastal water healthy again, the way it used to be before we humans upset the balance of nature."

"Oh! Do you mean before people caught too many big fish? Kelfie, the Kelp Elf, says there aren't enough big fish left to eat the sea urchins. Now the urchins are destroying the kelp forest!"

"Yes," Carly said, "but who is Kelfie?"

"He's a friend of mine. We talked through a magic shell in the garden today."

Carly smiled and said, *"Well, he's right!"* She chuckled to herself, amazed at Alani's wild imagination. *"The Bluebelt is going to be like the 'Greenbelt,' that your grandparents helped create to protect our open land areas. Here's a map that shows the Greenbelt,"* she said, and she spread it out on the table.

"We've marked the location we'd like to save as a Bluebelt. It's also called a 'Marine Protected Area,' or 'MPA'."

"I see," Alani pondered... " 'Greenbelt' to protect the land and 'Bluebelt' to protect the ocean." Looking closer, she pointed to the red arrow and said, "Kelfie must live right here... and the garden is above it."

Before Carly could answer, Alani asked, *"Can I PLEASE go to the meeting with you?"*

"Really? Of course! I'm glad you care so much about saving Kelfie's home. You know, the balance of nature has been disturbed in many habitats around the world. If the Bluebelt Protection Plan works here, it could be a model for other cities to follow."

23

The next afternoon Alani got back to the garden as fast as she could. Waiting anxiously for the necklace to appear on the stump, she saw a motion in the vines. Expecting Kelfie, she was surprised to hear,

"Meow!"

Alani lifted the vines. There was Alley Cat sitting at the top of some stairs Alani hadn't noticed yesterday.

"Wow," she said to Alley, *"If you can climb in here, so can I."*

... but, as she stepped down inside, her foot slipped,
and she slid faster and faster... down... down... down
the tunnel until she bumped into a boulder by the
edge of a saltwater pond.

"Ouch!" Alani cried. She tried to stand up, but her ankle was badly hurt.
"What?! Stuck in an underground tunnel?! How will I tell Mom? How will I get out?"

Just then Kelfie burst out of the water. Since he was invisible to her
without the necklace, all she saw was a big SPLASH!

Before she realized it was Kelfie, the magic necklace hung around her neck, and she heard him say, *"You will not be able to climb back up with that swollen ankle. If you come with me, I can make a bandage for you. Just like the shell's magic allows me to breathe on land, you will be able to breathe under water."*

28

Kelfie calmly said, *"Breathe normally."*

The next thing she knew, she was holding onto Kelfie's webbed hand as they dove into the pond. Alani was amazed that she had no trouble breathing under water.

They swam down through the tunnel into the light of the giant
kelp forest, weaving in and out of the swaying sea plants.

A few moments later they sat on a bed of green seagrass.

Resting on the ocean floor, Alani watched as Kelfie gently wrapped a leafy kelp stem around her ankle.

As she looked around, she understood what Kelfie had meant when he'd told her his forest was in trouble.

31

Alani saw that much of the kelp had broken away from the rocky seabed. The ocean floor was carpeted with thousands of spiny sea urchins. Because the ocean had been over-fished, there weren't enough predators to eat the urchins. Too many urchins ate the seaweed, so its holdfasts couldn't grasp onto the rocks anymore, and the giant kelp floated away.

Alani watched an Elf removing a fishhook from a large sea turtle's flipper. Another Elf was untangling a Garibaldi's tail from a plastic six-pack holder.

Just then a seal with sad eyes swam right up to Alani. A fishing line was wound around its neck, cutting into the skin of its throat.

Kelfie handed her a sharp shell, and together they cut the nylon that was choking the seal and set her free. Alani and Kelfie laughed as the seal and her gleeful pups performed an underwater ballet to thank them.

Now that Alani's ankle was wrapped, Kelfie motioned her to hold onto his hand again. They swam back to the cave opening and up the underwater tunnel.

From there, he was able to lead her carefully up the steps where they sat beneath the vine-covered dome in the garden.

"My ankle doesn't hurt anymore!" exclaimed Alani. *"Thank you, Kelfie."*

"You are very welcome! The seaweed wrap is an excellent healer."

"Now I see how badly you need our help," Alani said. "And I have good news for you... The villagers are going to talk to our leaders next week about a plan to save your kelp forest. It will be called the Bluebelt Protection Plan. If it passes, there will be laws telling people to stop catching so many fish and keep trash and poisons out of the ocean!"

"So that means our home may be saved after all!" Kelfie exclaimed. "I just hope it is not too late. Grandfather said that our Elf Clan must leave tonight, at least, for a while. We are going to swim far across the sea to join other Elf tribes from around the world. Their coral, plankton and kelp habitats are dying too. We are all meeting to see if there is any way we can solve our problems."

"How long will you be gone?"

"I am not sure, but I will be the scout to see if our forest becomes healthy enough for us to return home. The magic shell will be on the stump when I get back. Remember to watch for it!"

Alani nodded, handed the necklace back to Kelfie and said goodbye. Her clothes were still wet and muddy, but that was nothing unusual, as she always got soaked from the hose and dirty from digging in her garden.

Worried that she might never see her Elf friend again, Alani climbed out of the tunnel. Kelfie slid back down the passageway to the kelp forest.

Back at his undersea home, Kelfie told his grandfather the news. Grandfather was very happy to hear that their forest might be saved one day, but there was no time to lose.

Kelfie stowed the necklace safely inside his woven seagrass basket. Then he swam out to help the younger Elves as they reluctantly left their homes for the long journey ahead.

The week went by slowly, but, finally, it was Tuesday night, time for the Bluebelt meeting at City Hall. The village leaders listened as people spoke up, one by one, about the importance of keeping the ocean healthy. Alani stood beside her mom, who was last to speak in favor of the Bluebelt Protection Plan.

As they turned to go back to their seats, Alani surprised everyone by stepping up and bravely speaking into the microphone, *"Thank you for listening to us talk about saving the giant kelp forest. If you say 'YES' to the plan, my friend Kelfie and his Kelp Elf Clan can come back to their homes again!"*

Everyone smiled and thought how cute it was that Alani had imaginary ocean friends.

Then the mayor spoke, *"Thank you, Alani. You are a brave girl to speak to the City Council about what is important to your heart. We need more citizens like you to help us make good decisions for our city."*

Back in their seats, Carly put her arm around Alani. *"I'm so proud of you!"* she whispered.

The crowd waited anxiously for the Council members to make their decision. Finally, they were ready, and they voted, one by one...

"YES!" for the Bluebelt Plan.

There was a burst of applause, and shouts of *"HOORAY!"* rang throughout the City Council Chambers.

The Laguna villagers, young and old, spilled out of City Hall, proud that their voices had been heard. Because they had never given up trying to protect the ocean, Laguna's giant kelp forest could begin to heal.

Alani wished she could tell Kelfie the good news right away, but she knew it would be a long time before he came back. The Kelp Elves were far out in the ocean meeting with other Elf clans from around the world.

No matter how long it took, though, she would keep an eye out for the magic necklace.

The next day, as Alani was picking strawberries from her family's plot, she overheard some adults saying, *"If we flatten this mound of vines, we could put another table and umbrella here."*

"Oh, no," Alani thought. *"If they cover up the tunnel, Kelfie can't bring the magic necklace to me. I won't be able to talk to him anymore!"*

As she worried, she spied two large oval stones on the hillside, and she had an idea.

Alani ran to the little garden shed and took out three small cans of paint and some paintbrushes. She brushed off the two big stones. They were heavy, but she found she could roll them a little. She covered them in white paint and brushed big blue circles on them with smaller black circles inside.

Just then, her parents came through the front gate with a picnic basket...

"Alani," her dad laughed, "you made those stones look like big eyes!"
"Yes," she beamed, "I want to make this mound look like an elf head. Can you pick
them up for me and put them here and here, please?"

Her dad placed the stones so the mound looked like a big face.

"Wow, what a good idea!" her parents agreed. "Let's finish him up!" They added spiky
garlic plants on top for hair and placed sliced wood stumps on either side for ears.
Alani thought for a second and said, "I think I'll call him Kelfie, the Garden Elf!"
Her parents smiled and winked at each other.

To Alani's great relief, there was no more talk of destroying the mound. Everyone loved the Garden Elf's big, smiling eyes that seemed to follow them as they worked, played, and picnicked there. Even passersby came in through the gate to admire him and enjoy the beautiful park.

Still, Alani was worried about Kelfie and his Elf Clan, knowing they were somewhere, miles out at sea. She crossed her fingers.

Would the Bluebelt Plan work?
Would she ever see him again?

Meanwhile, Kelfie and his Clan finally reached their destination, a coral reef far from inhabited islands. They had swum for months, sometimes catching rides on the backs of migrating whales and dolphins.

Now they sat with hundreds of other Sea Elves in an ancient underwater arena. Wearing nautilus shell necklaces to communicate with each other, they waited to hear from their leaders.

One by one, the Plankton, Coral, and Kelp Elf leaders spoke about the problems in their habitats. Just like Kelfie's Clan, the others were losing their homes, mostly because of pollution and over-fishing.

Grandfather was the last to speak. *"We are all facing the same problems. Even though we have tried to fix the damage, it gets worse every day. But there IS hope! Kelfie has spoken to a human girl through a magic nautilus shell. She says her village people are trying to find solutions as we speak!"*

"Hooray!" the Elves all shouted.

Grandfather continued, *"They will try to limit fishing and stop the pollution that is destroying our kelp forest. Laguna will become a Marine Protected Area. It may take years to find out if their plan works. Our Clan will wait here until we are sure it is safe to return to our homes. Kelfie will travel back there as our scout."*

The Elves all agreed to wait in the coral beds for Kelfie's report. If the Bluebelt Plan worked in Laguna Beach, there might be hope for other habitats too.

Days, weeks and months went by. Alani kept looking for the magic necklace to appear again in its familiar place, but, to her growing disappointment, it was never there.

"Maybe the Kelp Elves will never come back," she worried as she finished up the day's garden chores. It was her job now to water the Garden Elf, too. As she turned the hose on it, sunlight shone through the spray, creating miniature rainbows. She remembered, sadly, that there were rainbows just like them the first day she had met Kelfie. She turned off the water and rolled up the hose. When she was ready to leave,

Alani noticed a movement in the vines.

An invisible webbed hand was placing the magic necklace on the stump.

Seeing the nautilus shell, Alani whispered, *"Kelfie, you're back!"*

Quickly, she hung it around her neck, lifted the vines and peeked through the opening.

There was Kelfie again, looking happier than she'd ever seen him.
And there was a change inside the tunnel... Two nautilus shells,
much larger than the one on her necklace, were mounted on the
cave walls near the wooden ears of the Garden Elf.

"*H*ello, Alani!" Kelfie exclaimed. *"We are back in our homes. The big fish have returned to eat most of the sea urchins, so the giant kelp can grow healthy again. The water is much cleaner now, too, and we see fewer plastic bags and less trash floating in the ocean. The villagers must have passed the Bluebelt Plan."*

"Yes!" Alani replied. *"Your home is now in a Marine Protected Area, 'MPA' for short. And, there are new laws to stop people from polluting the ocean!"*

"Grandfather and I noticed something else, too. When we peeked above the kelp canopy, we could see an elf-looking face here. Was that your idea?"

"Uh-huh! I was worried that the tunnel opening might get covered up. I'm calling it Kelfie... after you! As long as it's here, we will be able to talk!"

"Actually," Kelfie said, *"that is the sad part. These big nautilus shells are here so we will not have to come all the way up the tunnel to listen for land news. It was always dangerous for us Elves to be out of the water, but now we can listen safely from our homes under the sea."*

"Oh," Alani nodded sadly, realizing this might be the last time she would ever see her Elf friend again. But she said bravely, *"I understand. Of course, I don't want you to be in any danger. I won't look for the necklace anymore."*

*"But Grandfather wants you to KEEP the necklace in case
we need to contact you again. Just because we have laws to
protect us NOW does not mean they will last forever. There
will always be those who want to change them. Some people
will not want to be told where they can fish or how tall their
buildings can be. Since we sea and land creatures cannot
speak for ourselves, we need smart, caring people, like you,
to keep an eye out for changes in the laws and speak for us."*

"So now," he told Alani, *"when you hold the shell up
to your ear, you will hear the sound of ocean waves. If
that is ALL you hear, you will know that the kelp forest is
healthy. The magic nautilus shell will let me talk to you
again if we need your help."*

Alani smiled, proud to be entrusted with the precious
shell. *"I'll always treasure it and keep it in a safe place!"*
Then she added, *"Oh! I almost forgot to tell you... Earth
Day is coming up, and there will be festivals in Laguna to
celebrate our Greenbelt and Bluebelt. One of the parties
will be here, and our Garden Band will be playing. Do you
think your Clan will be able to hear us?"*

*"Yes! These two nautilus shells will carry the music all the
way down the tunnel to the kelp beds. We can celebrate
with you ANY time the gardeners have a party."*

50

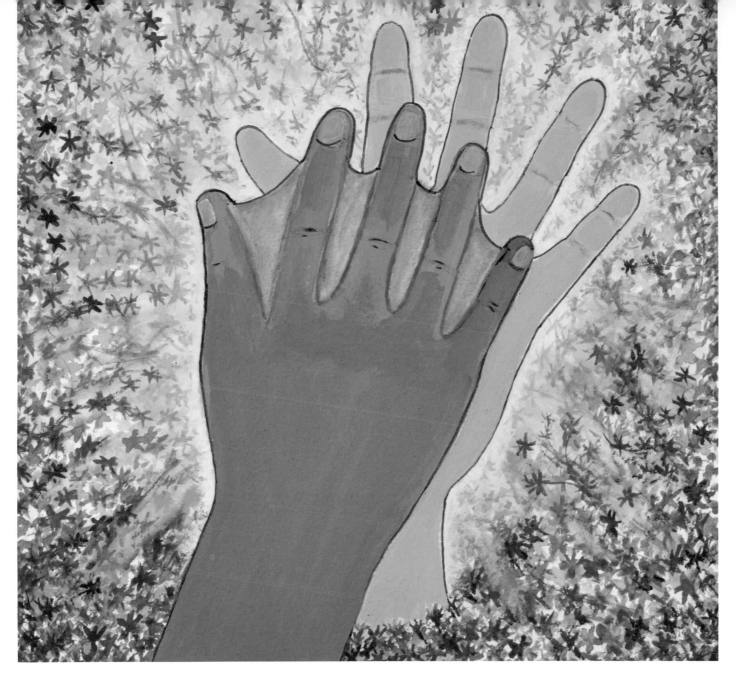

Alani knew her time with Kelfie had to end now, so she reached her hand out for a "high five" and said, *"Good-bye, Kelfie. I'll miss you!"*

"Good-bye, Alani!" Kelfie said, as he placed his webbed hand against hers. *"Thank you for being such a good friend!"*

At last, the day of the party arrived. Alani and her family danced with the other villagers to the rocking beat of the Garden Band. Everyone was in high spirits to celebrate Earth Day.

However, Alani was the only one who knew about the underwater party going on at the same time...

... Joining the celebration with their turtle-bop drums, shell shakers and coral flutes, the Kelp Elves danced to the rhythm of the garden music.

Thanks to the Laguna villagers, the kelp forest was now protected by the Bluebelt Plan.

That night Alani sat on her bed and looked out her window. She imagined the moonlight shining down through the giant kelp canopy to the sea floor, where the Elves were sleeping peacefully.

Picking up the nautilus shell and holding it to her ear, she heard the sound of ocean waves...

and that was all she heard.

Alani thought, *"All is well... for now."*

The End

for now...

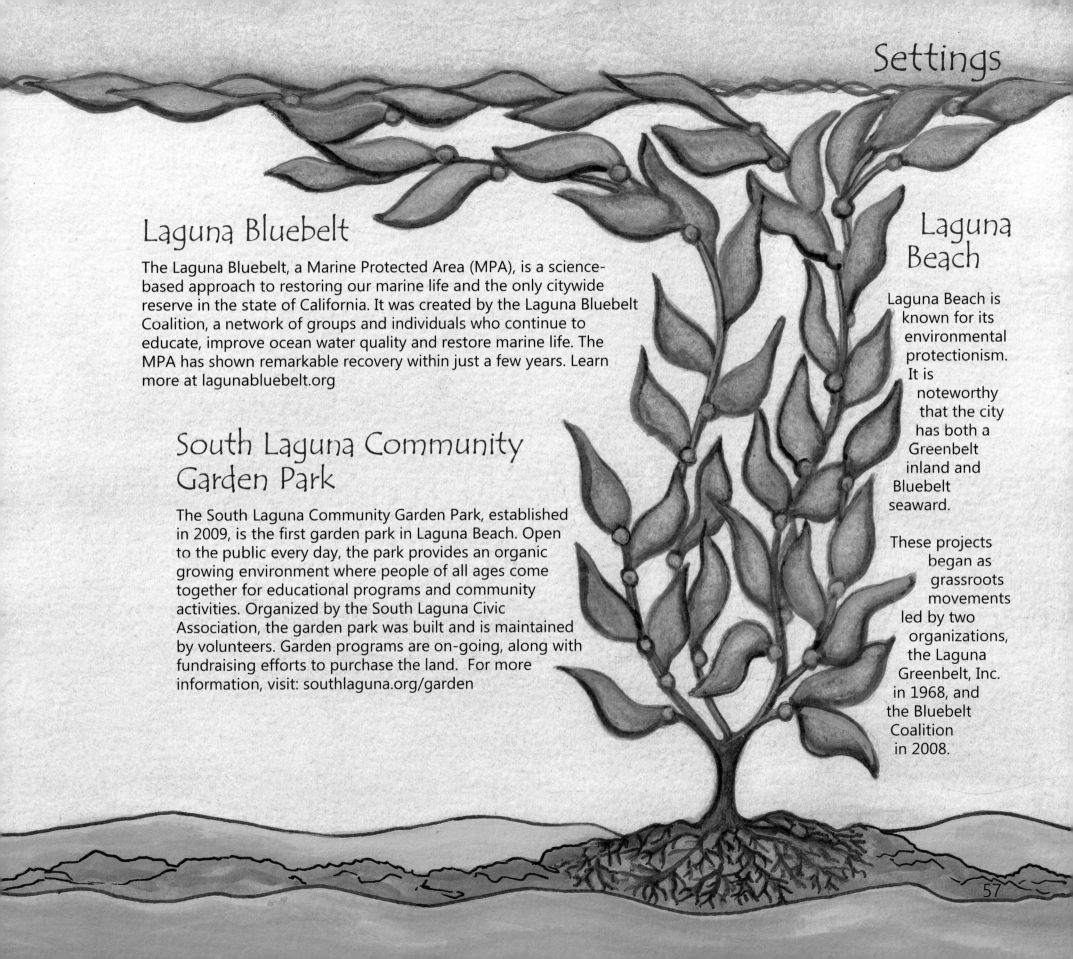

Laguna Bluebelt

The Laguna Bluebelt, a Marine Protected Area (MPA), is a science-based approach to restoring our marine life and the only citywide reserve in the state of California. It was created by the Laguna Bluebelt Coalition, a network of groups and individuals who continue to educate, improve ocean water quality and restore marine life. The MPA has shown remarkable recovery within just a few years. Learn more at lagunabluebelt.org

South Laguna Community Garden Park

The South Laguna Community Garden Park, established in 2009, is the first garden park in Laguna Beach. Open to the public every day, the park provides an organic growing environment where people of all ages come together for educational programs and community activities. Organized by the South Laguna Civic Association, the garden park was built and is maintained by volunteers. Garden programs are on-going, along with fundraising efforts to purchase the land. For more information, visit: southlaguna.org/garden

Laguna Beach

Laguna Beach is known for its environmental protectionism. It is noteworthy that the city has both a Greenbelt inland and Bluebelt seaward.

These projects began as grassroots movements led by two organizations, the Laguna Greenbelt, Inc. in 1968, and the Bluebelt Coalition in 2008.

57

Glossary

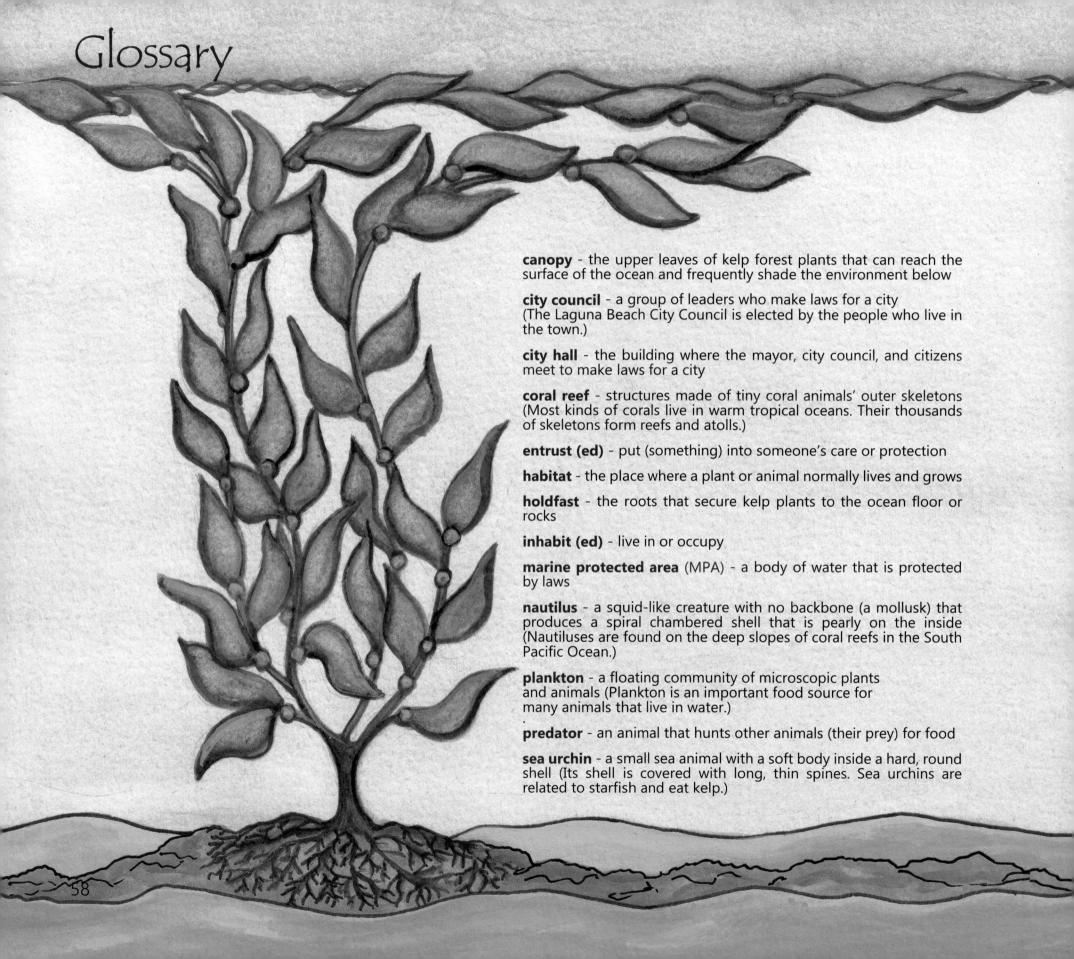

canopy - the upper leaves of kelp forest plants that can reach the surface of the ocean and frequently shade the environment below

city council - a group of leaders who make laws for a city (The Laguna Beach City Council is elected by the people who live in the town.)

city hall - the building where the mayor, city council, and citizens meet to make laws for a city

coral reef - structures made of tiny coral animals' outer skeletons (Most kinds of corals live in warm tropical oceans. Their thousands of skeletons form reefs and atolls.)

entrust (ed) - put (something) into someone's care or protection

habitat - the place where a plant or animal normally lives and grows

holdfast - the roots that secure kelp plants to the ocean floor or rocks

inhabit (ed) - live in or occupy

marine protected area (MPA) - a body of water that is protected by laws

nautilus - a squid-like creature with no backbone (a mollusk) that produces a spiral chambered shell that is pearly on the inside (Nautiluses are found on the deep slopes of coral reefs in the South Pacific Ocean.)

plankton - a floating community of microscopic plants and animals (Plankton is an important food source for many animals that live in water.)

predator - an animal that hunts other animals (their prey) for food

sea urchin - a small sea animal with a soft body inside a hard, round shell (Its shell is covered with long, thin spines. Sea urchins are related to starfish and eat kelp.)

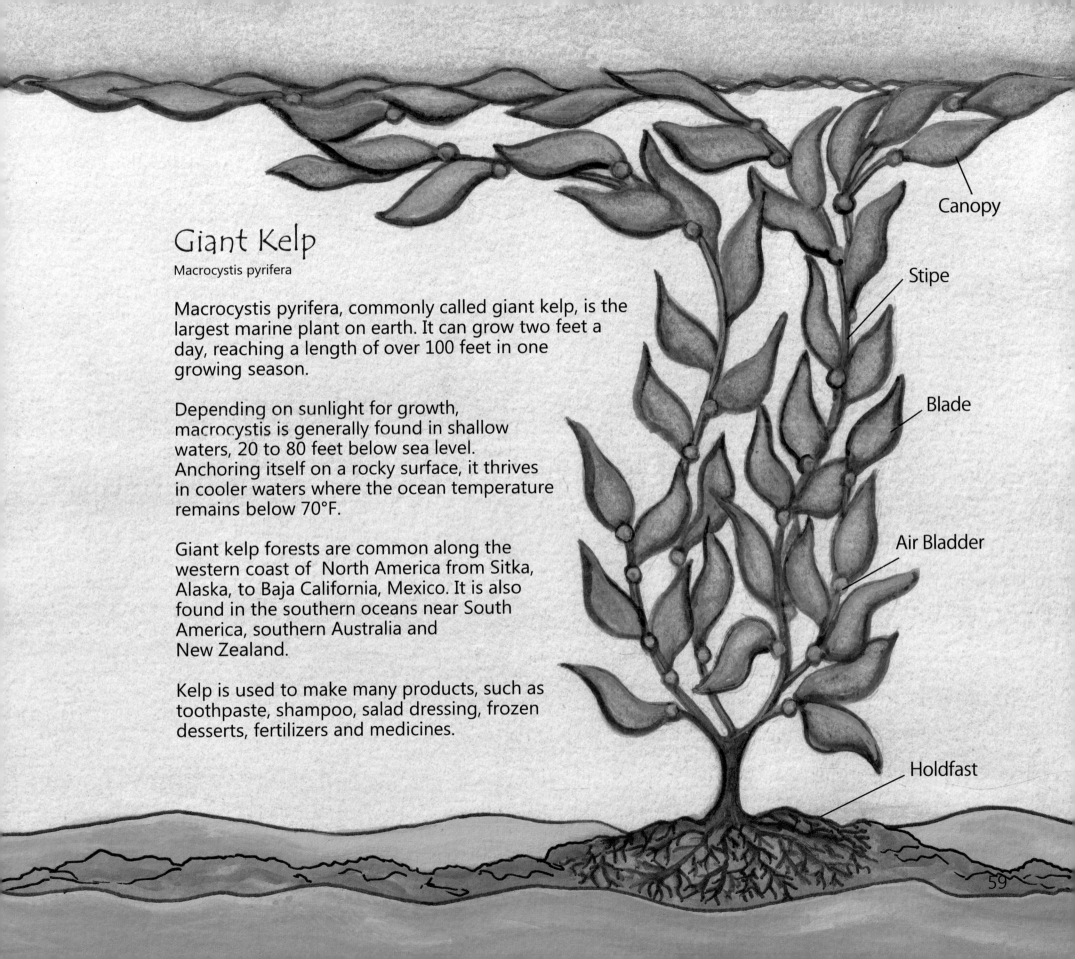

Giant Kelp

Macrocystis pyrifera

Macrocystis pyrifera, commonly called giant kelp, is the largest marine plant on earth. It can grow two feet a day, reaching a length of over 100 feet in one growing season.

Depending on sunlight for growth, macrocystis is generally found in shallow waters, 20 to 80 feet below sea level. Anchoring itself on a rocky surface, it thrives in cooler waters where the ocean temperature remains below 70°F.

Giant kelp forests are common along the western coast of North America from Sitka, Alaska, to Baja California, Mexico. It is also found in the southern oceans near South America, southern Australia and New Zealand.

Kelp is used to make many products, such as toothpaste, shampoo, salad dressing, frozen desserts, fertilizers and medicines.

Canopy

Stipe

Blade

Air Bladder

Holdfast

Kelp Forest Creatures

Giant kelp is home to over 800 species of animals who depend on it for food and shelter or as a hunting ground for prey. Ranging in size from microscopic to gigantic, these creatures include mammals, such as seals, sea otters and dolphins; invertebrates, like snails, seahares and octopi; hundreds of fish species; and birds. Even whales sometimes pass through the forests along their migrating routes.

Sculpin

Harbor Seal

Treefish

Opaleye

Senorita

Kelp Crab

Red Octopus

Bat Star

Spiny Lobster

60

Garibaldi
(California State fish)

Surf Perch

Green
Sea Turtle

Giant Sea Bass

Sheephead
(female)

Sheephead
(male)

Kelp Bass

Bat Ray

Sea Urchins

Sea Anemones

Abalone

Ochre Sea Star

Environmental Organizations in and around Laguna Beach

Crystal Cove Alliance (crystalcovebeachcottages.org)

Laguna Bluebelt Coalition (lagunabluebelt.org)

Laguna Canyon Conservancy (Facebook)

Laguna Canyon Foundation (lagunacanyon.org)

Laguna Greenbelt (lagunagreenbelt.org)

Laguna Ocean Foundation (lagunaoceanfoundation.org)

One World One Ocean (oneworldoneocean.com)

Orange County Coastkeeper (coastkeeper.org)

Pacific Marine Mammal Center (pacificmmc.org)

Sierra Club (sierraclub.org)

South Laguna Civic Association (southlaguna.org)

South Laguna Community Garden Park (southlaguna.org/garden)

Surfrider International (surfrider.org)

Transition Laguna Beach (transitionlagunabeach.org)

Village Laguna (villagelaguna.org)

References

Books

Chilcote, Ronald H. 2014. **The Laguna Wilderness**. Laguna Wilderness Press

McPeak, Ronald H. and Dale A. Glantz and Carole R. Shaw. 1988. **The Amber Forest**. Watersport Publishing, Inc.

Websites

Laguna Bluebelt Coalition (lagunabluebelt.org)

South Laguna Community Garden Park (southlaguna.org/garden)

Acknowledgments

The authors wish to thank all the thoughtful and creative people who contributed to this book, especially: Mike Beanan, Lynette Brasfield, Beverley Brezden, Ann Christoph, Nelson Coates, John Davey, Lila Davey, Ruben Flores, Jeff Haynes, Michelle Haynes, Katie Lang-Slattery, Charlotte Masarik, Elizabeth McGhee, Lu Neely, Ginger Osborne, Tom Osborne, Elaine Reames, Alani Sciacca, Carly Sciacca, Jinger Wallace, Sue Webber, and Carole Zavala.

Gayle and Tom Joliet
authors/illustrators

Longtime Laguna Beach residents, Gayle and Tom Joliet, build upon their years of experience as public school teachers and practicing artists to create this informative, entertaining tale for children.
It is their way of expressing appreciation for the Laguna Beach villagers whose tireless grassroots efforts led to the creation of both the "Greenbelt" and "Bluebelt".

Gayle and Tom have traveled extensively, leading to their deep reverence for the land, the sea and all its inhabitants. As environmental advocates, the Joliets give back to their community by volunteering at the South Laguna Garden Park, Laguna Beach Public Radio, and the Susi Q Community Center.

The goal of this children's book is to inspire today's youth to conserve and restore native habitats, preserving the diversity of life for future generations.

ALANi and the Giant Kelp Elf
Published by LAGUNA WILDERNESS PRESS

©2019 LAGUNA WILDERNESS PRESS

Illustrations and text ©2019 Gayle and Tom Joliet

ISBN: 9780984000760
LIBRARY OF CONGRESS: 2019943745
DESIGN BY: Charles Michael Murray
PRINTED IN PRC BY IMAGO

LAGUNA WILDERNESS PRESS
PO BOX 5703
LAGUNA BEACH, CA 92652-0149

TEL: 951 827 1571
EMAIL: orders@LagunaWildernessPress.com
WEB: LagunaWildernessPress.com
FACEBOOK: facebook.com/lagunawildernesspress

The Laguna Wilderness Press is a non-profit press dedicated to publishing books concerned with the presence, preservation and importance of wilderness environments.

Chilcote, Ronald H.
The Laguna Wilderness
Laguna Wilderness Press
2014

Robert L. Allen & Fred M. Roberts Jr.
Wildflowers of Orange County and the Santa Ana Mountains
Laguna Wilderness Press
2013

Allan A. Schoenherr
Wild and Beautiful
Laguna Wilderness Press
2011